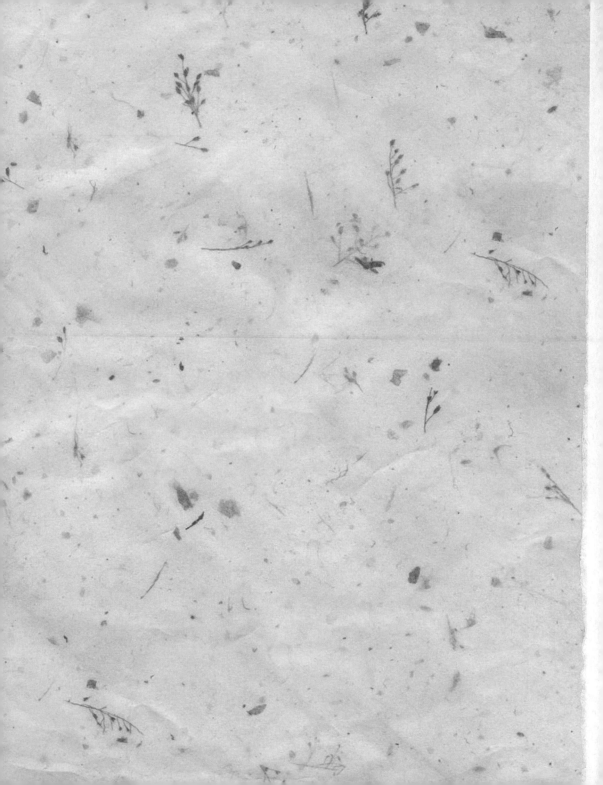

MOUSE
BIRD
SNAKE
WOLF

MOUSE

First U.S. edition 2013

Library of Congress Catalog Card Number 2012950556
ISBN 978-0-7636-5912-7

13 14 15 16 17 18 SCP 10 9 8 7 6 5 4 3 2 1

Printed in Humen, Dongguan, China.

This book was typeset in Priori Serif.
The illustrations were done in mixed media.

Candlewick Press
99 Dover Street
Somerville, Massachusetts 02144

visit us at www.candlewick.com

CANDLEWICK PRESS

David Almond

Bird

Illustrated by
Dave McKean

SNAKE

WOLF

For Dave and Sue
D. A.

For Lexie and Emily
D. M.

Long ago and far away, in a world rather like this
one, and with people in it rather like us, there were
three children: **Harry, Sue** and **Ben.**

Ben was known as
Little Ben, because
he was so small.

Like many worlds, the world
they lived in was a marvellous
place filled with marvellous things.
It was safe and calm and rather
wonderful. But it was a strange
old place as well. There were
gaps and holes in it. There were
places where there seemed to be
nothing at all, places that were
filled with emptiness.

Some of these were
huge as deserts;
some were no bigger
than a fingernail.

The trouble was, the gods who had made the world had become rather fat and rather too pleased with themselves. Oh yes, they had worked great wonders in days gone by.

They had made mighty mountains, tender flowers, rivers, forests, seas!

They had made astounding animals: the elephant, the camel, the whale ...

and man and woman, of course, and babies and children ...

and beasts that we in our world have no names for.

But now, they spent day after day lying on their clouds, sipping tea together, and nibbling sandwiches and cakes. They chatted about their creations, and gazed down at them with deepest fondness.

"*Your elephant, sir, is a thing of wonder!*"
one would say to another.
   "*Ah yes, indeed, but what about your chain of
mountains, and your sparkling ponds and streams!*"
   "*But each time I see your wisteria, my eyes fill
with tears. Such restraint, such delicacy.
Oh, and those sweet daisies …*"

"But your humpback whale!
Such magnificence!"
   "And your extraordinary zowet!"
   "Your gazelle!"
   "Oh, but your brant!"

   And they would shrug and blush and lower their eyes.

   They'd be silent for a time; then one would whisper, *"Could any other gods
come up with anything more astonishing?"*

And one would answer, "No. *There are no other worlds like this one. There are no other gods like us. We are indeed the best of all gods in the best of all worlds.*" And they would all smile in agreement.

And so they lay on their clouds, and floated through
the sky, and took tea, and slept and snored. And yes,
they did tell one another what they would make once
they got back to work, if only they had the energy,
and if only they had the time, but in truth their world
was still unfinished, still had many gaps and spaces in
it, and there was still much making to be done.

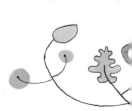

One day, Harry, Sue and Little Ben decided to go wandering. Not too far — just through the fields and woods around their homes. They walked on walls, climbed over fences, jumped across streams, swung from trees. They dared one another to dash and leap through empty spaces — which could be a little scary, but great fun.

After a while, they lay down on soft turf beneath a gnarled old tree and beside a sparkling stream and they rested.

All of a sudden, Little Ben said in surprise, as if he'd never thought of it before, *"This is a very peculiar world!"*

He looked up at the clouds.

"Why are there so many gaps and spaces in it?" he yelled.

The gods took no notice.

"It needs more things in it!" he said.

Still no notice.

Little Ben sighed. *"Have you ever looked into an empty space?"* he asked his friends.

"Of course we have," they said.
"Sometimes," Little Ben continued, *"when you look into an empty space, you can kind of see something in it."*

Harry shook his head. Sue rolled her eyes.

"*Yes!*" said Ben. "*It's a mousy thing …*

a funny little squeaky scampery thing."
   "*Then it's just like you!*" said Harry.

"*Yes!*" Ben laughed. And he thought of a mouse inside himself.

"Tell you what,"
he said.
*"I'll show you what
one looks like.
Watch."*

He glanced
up into the sky.

The gods weren't looking.

He gathered
some wool and
some petals
and some nuts
and made the
shape of a
mouse with
them. He laid it
in the grass.

"*Squeak and scamper, little mouse,*" he whispered.

"*Come along.*

Don't be shy. Squeak and scamper."

The children laughed.

They didn't really believe that the mouse would squeak and scamper, but as they watched, it started to tremble and wake.
"*Oh, look!*" Sue cried.
"*What a lovely little thing it is!*"

The mouse tottered to its tiny feet; it sniffed the air; it peeped into the sky with its little bright eyes.

It squeaked, and squeaked again, and squeaked again, and scampered right away.

The children clapped their hands.

"*It seemed quite at home!*" Harry said.

Ben giggled. "*At last!*" he exclaimed. "*This is a world with a mouse in it, thanks to me!*"

And the children lay on the grass and thought
of the mouse running through the fields and
forests and the empty spaces and through their
minds and they were very pleased.

And the gods? They hardly seemed to stir at all.

After a time, Sue said,
"Now I will have a turn."

She looked
into the sky.
She looked
into herself.

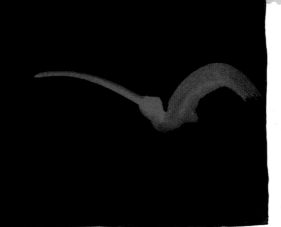

"I think," she said, "that what this world needs next is a ... bird!"

The gods rolled over in their sleep and gentle thunder sounded.

"A bird?" asked Harry. "What kind of thing is a bird, Sue?"

"A bird," said Sue, "is a kind of birdy thing, of course.

It's a thing that … sings!
And … flaps its wings!
And it … flies!
Yes, that's it! It flies through the empty air!"

The others giggled.

"You're just making that up!" said Harry.

"Of course I am," said Sue.

"And surely," said Little Ben, "there couldn't possibly be a creature like that! Could there?"

"Yes, there could," said Sue. "Just watch!"

So she collected some sticks and she gathered some leaves and she picked some grass and she made a bird with them.

She cradled it in her hands and held it up to the sky.

"This will never work!" said Harry.

"Sing, bird! Sing!" said Sue.

*"Come along.
Sing, bird, sing!"*

And as the children
watched, the bird
opened its eyes and
its small sharp beak
and it sang the
sweetest of songs.

"Oh!" they
gasped.

*"That is so
beautiful, Sue!"*
said Little Ben.

"That is nothing," she said. "Just watch!"

She held the singing bird close to her face. "Now, little bird," she whispered. "Fly! Go on. Flap your wings. Fly away!"

Nothing happened, so she said it again. And the bird trembled in her fingers, and she said it again: "Fly, little bird. Fly!"

And the bird kept on trembling and singing, and Sue said it all again, and said it all again, and the children chewed their lips in excitement, and at last the bird opened its wings and leapt from Sue's hands into the empty air and it flew once, twice, three times, around their heads and then right away and out of sight.

The children
goggled and
giggled and
gasped.
They were
speechless.

"Oh, Sue," Little Ben said at last. "The thing
called a bird is simply wonderful! What a marvellous
thing to have in the world!"

They clapped their hands and stamped their
feet and the ground shook with their excitement.

High above, one of the gods opened his eyes.

He rolled over, and looked down from his
cloud. He smiled at the children having such fun.

He saw the bird, flitting across the world.
What a pretty thing! he thought.
How on earth did that get there?
He glanced at the other gods.
Maybe they'd been working while he'd
been fast asleep. But it didn't look like it.
He shrugged.
Anyway, he thought,
it's very clever.

Then he yawned, and closed his eyes
again, and went back to his dreams.

Little Ben and Sue turned to Harry.

"Now," Sue said. "What
will you make, Harry?"
"Me?"
"Yes, you," said Ben.
"Everyone must have a
turn," said Sue.

Harry wondered. He walked
and the others walked alongside.

He stared into
the wide sky
and wondered.

He stared at
the dark earth
and wondered.

He stared into the forests and
into the empty spaces of the
world and wondered.

He closed his eyes
and stared into himself.

"*Yes!*" he said at last. "*I shall make a snake!*"

A god opened her eyes wide and looked down.

"*A snake?*" said the others.

Harry smiled. "*Yes. A snake. It is a most peculiar thing. It is a long and twisty legless thing. It has a forked little tongue and sharp little teeth. It hisses, and it slithers across the earth.*"

"*Goodness gracious,*" said Sue. "*What a weird creature!*"

"Now, watch," ordered Harry. *"This will be very simple."*

He grabbed some clay from a little pond. He found some shining stones in the soil. He made a snake with them and laid it on the ground at their feet.

"*Slither, snake! Slither!*" he urged.
"*Hiss, snake! Hiss!*"

But nothing happened.

"*Try again,*" said Sue and Little Ben.
"*Try harder, Harry.*"

Harry took a deep breath. He looked up at the clouds. The god glared at him; the god shook her head at him.

Harry took no notice. He tried to feel as a god feels when she is making things.

He tried to feel as a snake feels when it is being made.

"*Hiss!*" he hissed.
"*Slither!*" he hissed.
He twisted his body and
flicked his tongue.
"*Ssss!*" he hissed.
"*Ssss! Ssss! Ssss!*"

And yes!
The snake hissed.

It lifted its head
and it hissed again.

It slithered towards them across the grass.
Its scales glittered. Its eyes gleamed.
It bared its sharp little teeth. It flicked its forked little tongue.

The children backed away and backed away and Ben held tight to Harry and Sue. And then the snake discovered a crack in the ground and it slithered fast into the earth below.

The children goggled.
"*Golly!*" Sue gasped.
"*Goodness gracious! What a thing!*"
And they were very quiet for a time.

"*Perhaps,*" said Little Ben at last, "*we've made enough for today. Perhaps we should have a rest, like the gods do.*"

And the god looked down and nodded. *"Yes,"* she said. *"Have a rest, like the gods do, before you do something silly."*

They did try, and Little Ben almost fell asleep, as he did most afternoons because he was still so small. And they lay there on the ground in the sunshine, just as the gods lay on the clouds above. And they thought of the things they had made, just as the gods did, and were extremely pleased with themselves, just as the gods were.

But Sue couldn't keep still, and Harry couldn't keep quiet.

"I don't want to have a rest," he said.

"Nor do I," said Sue.

They stood up straight and they stared across the earth and they stared into their minds and they searched their thoughts and they searched their dreams and they wondered.

They started to walk, and to talk as quickly as they walked.

"Listen," said Sue. *"What we need now is a thing called a wolf."*

"A wolf?" said Little Ben, *who had to hurry to keep up.*

"Yes," said Harry. *"Sue's right. We absolutely definitely need a wolf."*

"What in the world is a wolf?" asked Ben.

"Oh," said Harry. *"A wolf is very, very wolfy."*

"It is a great big hairy thing with a … great big head!" said Sue.

"That's right," agreed Harry. "And it has great big massive teeth."

"And long strong legs and ... great big paws," said Sue.

"And it howls really, *really* loud," said Harry.

"And it runs really, really, *really fast*," said Sue.

"*Oh, it's a wonderful thing*," they cried.

Little Ben said,
"*But isn't that a bit ...?*"
He scratched his head,
as if he didn't know
the word he was
looking for.
"*A bit scary*,"
he said at last.

"*No!*" said Harry and
Sue.

"*Isn't it a bit ...
dangerous?*"

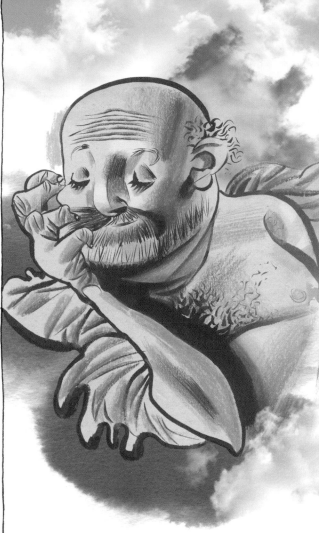

"*Of course not!*" said Harry. "*Don't be silly. Don't be scared. A wolf is a wonderful, beautiful, marvellous thing.*"

And they stood still and stared up into the clouds and Sue yelled, "*Isn't it? Isn't a wolf a wonderful, beautiful, marvellous thing?*"

And the one god who heard them looked down and smiled, and shrugged, and muttered, "*Yes, children. I suppose it is.*" And fell fast asleep.

"See?"
said Harry.

"See?"
said Sue.

"*Hmm*,"
said Little
Ben.

Harry found some clay;
Sue fetched some wool.
Harry collected some big
sticks; Sue gathered some
big stones. They got some
petals and nuts and grass.
They made a wolf. There it
was, lying on the ground
beside them, waiting to be
called.

Little Ben
watched the wolf.
He walked towards
a nearby tree.
"If you don't mind,"
he said. *"I think
I'll climb
this tree."*
And up
he went.

"Silly boy,"
said Harry
and Sue.

They turned
to the wolf.
   "*Howl!*" said Harry.
   "*Run!*" said Sue.

Nothing happened.
   "*HOWL!*"
shouted Harry.
   "*RUN!*"
yelled Sue.

Nothing happened.
   "*Shall we stop now?*"
said Ben up the tree.
   "*No!*" said Harry.
   "*We just need to try harder,*"
said Sue.
   So they tried harder.

They tried to feel as a god feels when he is making things.
They tried to feel as a wolf feels when it is being made.
They raised their voices as if they were howling.

They drummed their feet as if they were running.

"HOWL, WOLF, HOWL!" they howled.

"RUN, WOLF, RUN!" they howled.

They woke a god, and he sat up and dangled his feet over the edge of his cloud and wagged his finger in warning. *"This is a job for the gods!"* he scolded. *"Not for silly little children like you."* But the children took no notice, and the god looked down in fascination as they snarled and drooled and yelped, and the ground trembled as they raced in circles around the wolf.

"OWOWOWOWOOOOO!" they yelled.

"OWOWOWOOOOOOO!"

And yes, the wolf stirred!

And yes, it stood up!
And yes, it howled!
And yes, it ran!

It howled and it ran
straight at Harry and
Sue ...

And it gobbled them up.

Then it howled
once more and lay
on the ground and
fell fast, fast asleep.

The god clicked his tongue
and shook his head.
"What silly children," he said.
*"What a very, very silly
thing to do."*

And Little Ben said,
"Golly! Goodness gracious …

What a weird
peculiar thing!"

He climbed down from the tree.

Gently he touched the wolf.
It was such a mighty thing and
he was Little Ben, so small.
He stared at the wolf and he
wondered.

He stared into himself
and he wondered.
He looked up at the
god looking down
and he wondered.

"*What can I do?*" he asked.
The god just shrugged and said,
"*I did warn them, you know.*"

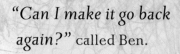

"*Can I make it go back again?*" called Ben.

The god stared into the sky. This was all very tiring, and it would soon be time for tea and cakes.

"*Can I unmake things as well as make them?*" shouted Ben. "*Can I turn the wolf back into clay and sticks and petals and nuts and grass?*"

The god yawned.

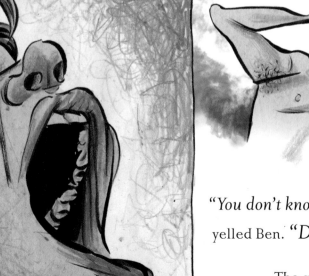

"*You don't know, do you?*" yelled Ben. "*DO YOU?*"

The god rolled over and closed his eyes.

Little Ben stamped his feet.
"Turn back again, wolf," he said.
Nothing happened.

*"TURN BACK AGAIN,
WOLF!"* he cried.
"Come on, Little Ben," he said
to himself. *"Try harder."*

He tried to feel as a god feels
when he is unmaking things.
He tried to feel as a wolf feels
when it is being unmade.
He tried to feel like clay and wool and sticks
and stones and petals and nuts and grass.
"TURN BACK AGAIN, WOLF!" he cried.

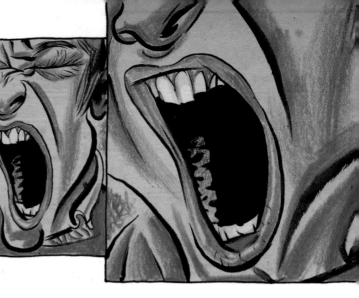

"TURN BACK AGAIN, WOLF!

*TURN BACK
AGAIN, WOLF!*"

And as he watched, the
wolf began to turn back,
and it turned to clay
and wool and sticks and
stones and petals and
nuts and grass.

And lying in the middle,
fast asleep, were Harry
and Sue.

"Thank goodness!" sighed Little Ben. He touched his friends. *"Wake up,"* he whispered. *"It's time to go home."*

And Harry and Sue sat up and yawned and stretched. They stepped out from the thing that had been their wolf.

"*I think we've made enough for now,*"
said Little Ben. "*Don't you?*"
Harry and Sue nodded.
"*I think we should go home now,*"
said Little Ben. "*Don't you?*"

Harry and Sue nodded again. They
were silent. They had been inside
their wolf; now their wolf was
inside them, like a dream.

They felt it, running through
them. They heard it, howling
and snarling deep inside
them.

Ben took their hands
and pulled them away.

They ran homeward quickly,
through the fields and the woods
and the empty spaces, across that
lovely, strange, unfinished world.

They were watched by a tiny mouse hunched
in the grass; by a lovely bird that soared in
the sky; by a flickery snake from a little dark
hole; and by the gods above, who were now
beginning to stir and wake.

"*Nice sleep?*" the gods asked one another.
"*Oh yes,*" they said. "*Oh certainly, oh definitely, oh yes.*"

"Cup of tea?" one asked. *"Piece of cake?"*
"Oh yes. Oh certainly definitely yes."

So they took tea and they nibbled cake.

And one god turned to another god and said,

"You know, I find that cake produces the most marvellous of dreams."

"It does indeed," said another. *"In my dream there was the prettiest little thing called a mouse. And you know, I think it is exactly what is needed in our world. I will make one tomorrow."*

"And I will make a very marvellous birdy thing called a bird," said another.

"And I a splendid, slippery, slithery snake," said a third.

"Anything else?" they asked. *"Were there any other dreams? Do we need anything else?"*

"Such as?"

"Well, a … wolfy thing, perhaps?" one muttered.

"Oh no," came an answer. *"Whatever that is, I don't think we have need of a thing like that."*

And they all agreed.

But then they fell silent, and there
came a sound from deep inside
themselves, and from the gaps
and spaces that they'd left below:
astonishing snarling, extraordinary
howling. And the gods listened and
were entranced, and they all knew, as
they sipped their tea and nibbled their
cake, that the new and marvellous
beast would soon find its way out
again into the world.

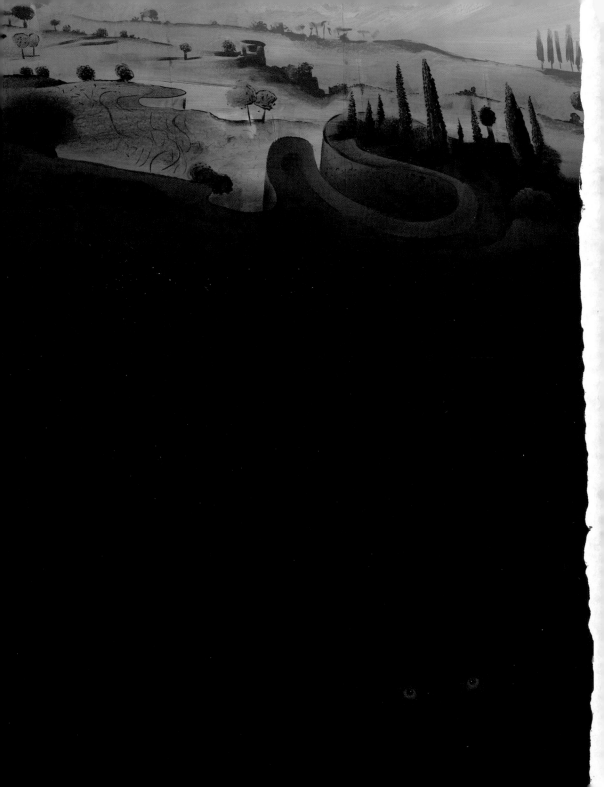

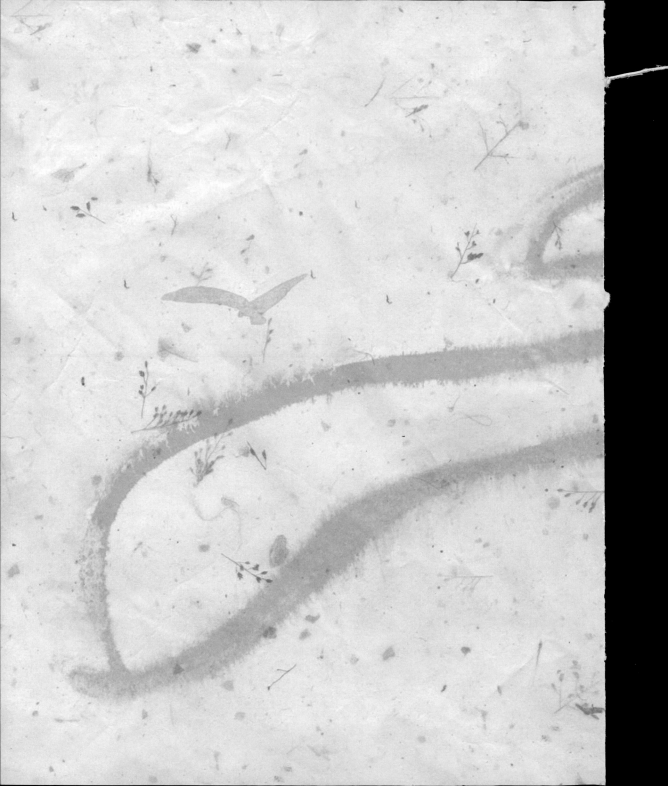